W9-ABD-832

Copyright © 1990 by Nord-Süd Verlag AG, Gossau Zürich, Switzerland
First published in Switzerland under the title *Sonne und Mond*
English translation copyright © 1990 by Rosemary Lanning

First published in the United States, Great Britain, Canada,
Australia, and New Zealand in 1990 by North-South Books,
an imprint of Nord-Süd Verlag AG, Gossau Zürich, Switzerland.
First paperback edition published in 1998.

Distributed in the United States by North-South Books Inc., New York.

Library of Congress Catalog Number: 89-43251
Library of Congress Cataloging-in-Publication Data is available.
A CIP catalogue record for this book is available from The British Library.
ISBN 1-55858-995-3 (paperback)
1 3 5 7 9 TB 10 8 6 4 2

Printed in Belgium

For more information about our books, and the authors and artists
who create them, visit our web site: http://www.northsouth.com

Marcus Pfister

Sun *and* Moon

TRANSLATED BY ROSEMARY LANNING

North-South Books
New York

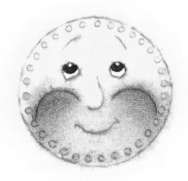

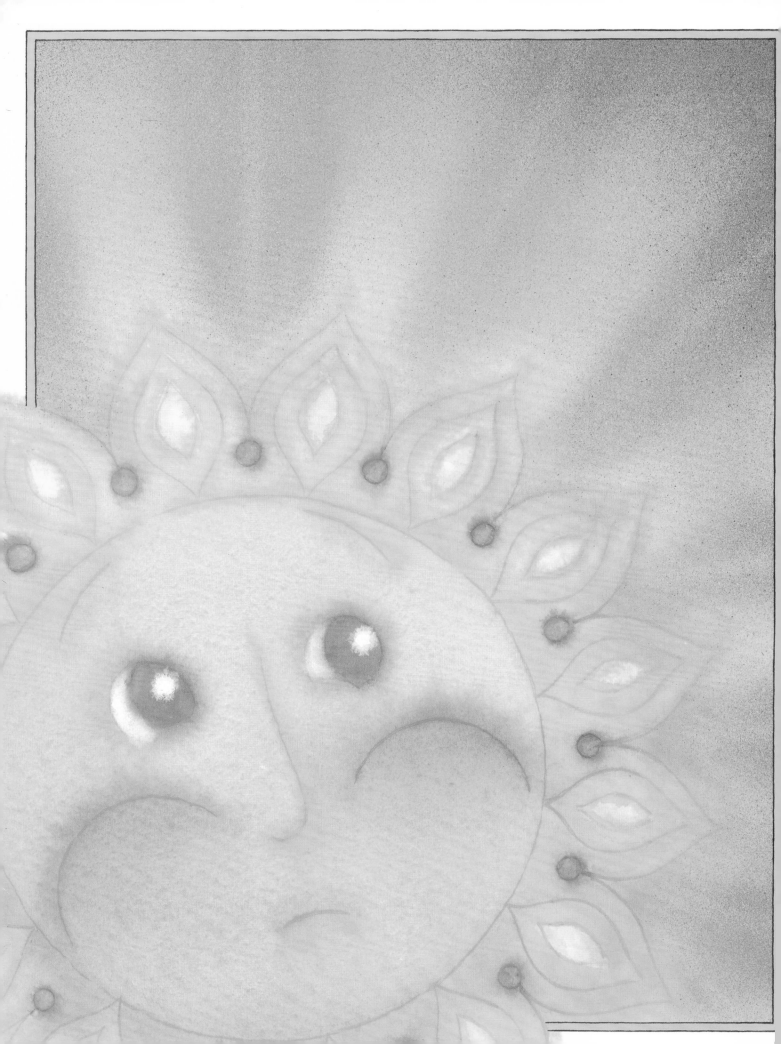

It was a bright autumn morning and the Sun was climbing high into the sky, but his face was sad as he gazed down on the Earth.

The Earth was worried. "What is the matter?" it asked, "You are drawing those clouds across your face as if you wanted to hide. And you look so unhappy."

"I feel lonely," answered the Sun. "I have followed the same path across the sky, day after day, for as long as I can remember, and have never found a friend. That's why I'm so sad."

"What about the Wind?" asked the Earth. "Couldn't he be your friend?"

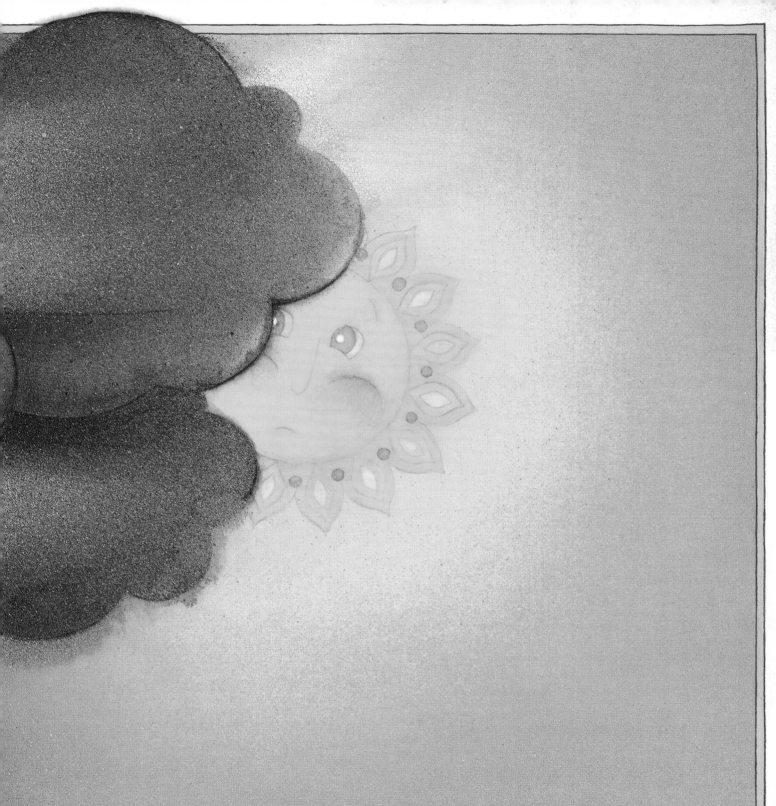

"No!" cried the Sun. "He teases me, darting around all the time and blowing clouds at my face. Not small clouds that look like fluffy little lambs, but dark storm clouds full of rain. Would a friend do that?"

"And thunderstorms really frighten me, booming and rumbling as they roll towards me, blinding me with flashes of lightning. They make little mice run into their holes, foxes creep into their dens and birds huddle down into their nests. Everyone is afraid of them—the children most of all."

"Then what about the Rainbow?"

The Sun smiled and said, "The Rainbow is a good friend. He comforts me when I'm struggling to break through the heavy rain clouds. But when the rain goes, so does the Rainbow and I'm even lonelier than before."

"Poor Sun," said the Earth. "But what about the children? Couldn't they be your friends? They're very fond of you."

"I like the children, too, but I can never get close enough to them. All I can do is tickle their noses. Then the children say, 'Atchoo!' and laugh. I can't laugh any more. I feel too lonely. Shining gives me no pleasure at all."

When evening came, the Sun veiled himself in mist and sank mournfully under the horizon.

Then the Moon appeared. She felt lonely too, after so many years alone in the vast, empty sky. And she also wished she had a friend to keep her company.

The Earth could see that the Moon was lonely too. "Don't be sad," said the Earth softly. "Aren't the Stars your friends?"

"I love the Stars," said the Moon. "But they are so far away that they can't hear me."

"But what about the Comets? They always like to play."

"I like the Comets," said the Moon with a smile. "But they rush past me so quickly that they often disappear before I can even say hello."

"And the children? Surely they could be your friends. They love to watch you shine in the night sky."

"I know. I know. They call me beautiful. They sing songs about the lovely Moon. But when I try to visit them, when I peek through their windows at night, they are fast asleep."

"Try not to be so sad, dear Moon. I'm sure you'll find a friend one day."

"I know who I'd like to be my friend," said the Moon. "Every morning, when night comes to an end, I gaze across at the Sun. I see him send out his first golden rays, and I always think he looks so handsome. Yes, he could be my very best friend."

Each morning the Sun glanced shyly at the silvery Moon, and also longed to make friends. But how could they ever meet? Would they have to disappear from the sky and go away somewhere?

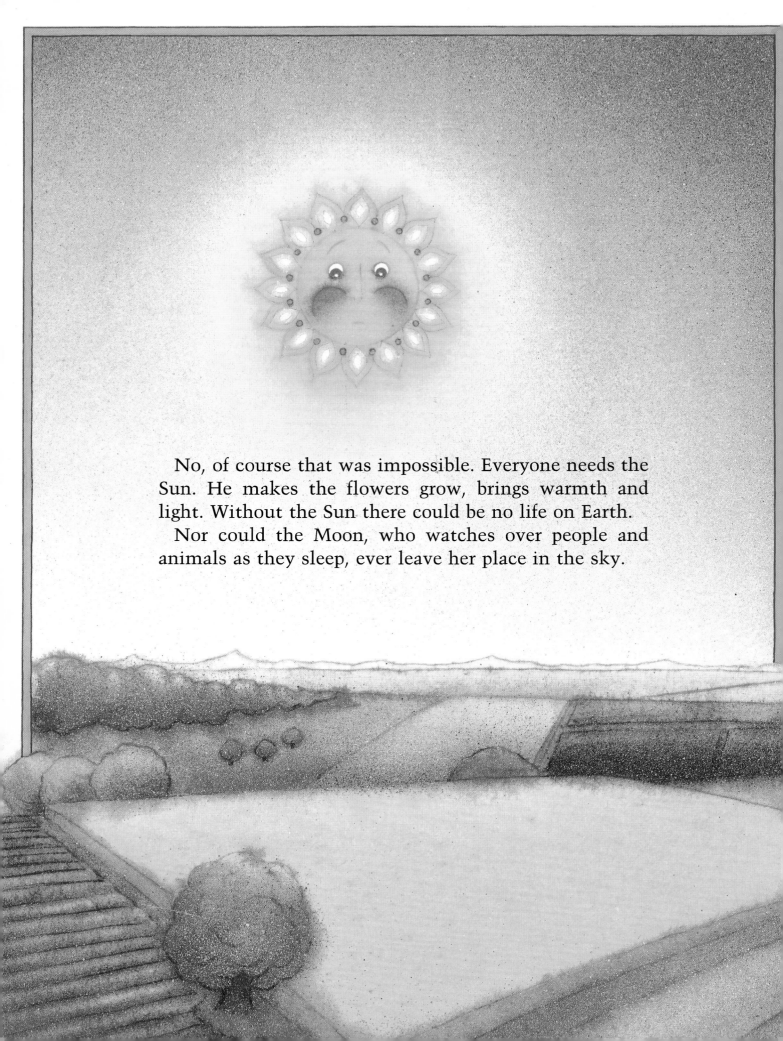

No, of course that was impossible. Everyone needs the Sun. He makes the flowers grow, brings warmth and light. Without the Sun there could be no life on Earth.

Nor could the Moon, who watches over people and animals as they sleep, ever leave her place in the sky.

Then suddenly one evening the Moon called out to the Sun.

"Let's be friends, dear Sun. We can talk every morning and every evening and tell each other about all the interesting things we've seen. Who knows, maybe one day our paths will even cross!"

When the Sun heard this he blushed with happiness and his light became more dazzling than ever.

Everyone was pleased that the Sun and the Moon were becoming friends. They looked so happy each time they spoke, and as time went on they moved closer and closer together.

One lovely, cloudless day the Moon finally moved in front of the Sun. The sky became very dark and all that could be seen of the Sun was a narrow fiery ring.

"The Sun is gone! It's a total eclipse!" cried the people, running around in great excitement. They fetched sheets of darkened glass so that they could look at this extraordinary event.

The Sun and the Moon couldn't stay together very long because they knew that the people and animals depended on them—night and day.

But the two friends decided to meet regularly from then on. They always look forward to their next meeting and are much happier now that they have found friendship at last.

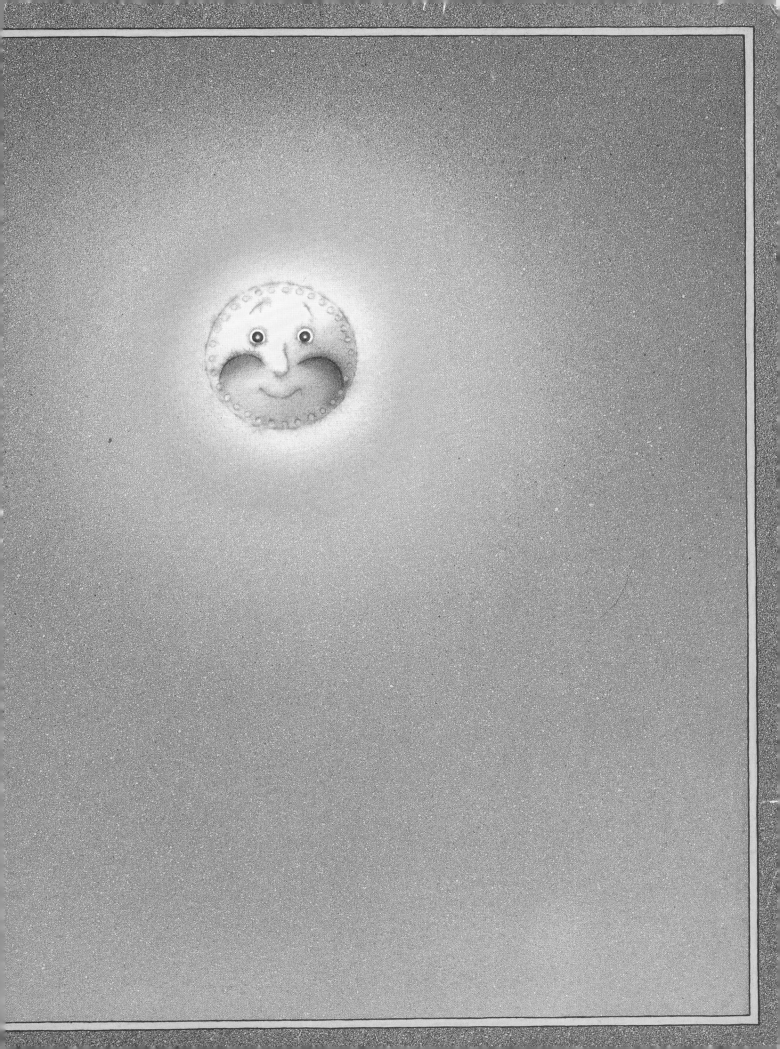